For Lila,

Here's a place to keep track of
your gymnastics goals and progress.
I believe in you!

Your coach and friend,
McKenna

This journal belongs to:

Lila Maria Monetti

2024

American Girl.

I can't believe McKenna gave me this journal! She used to be my babysitter, but now she's my gymnastics coach.

Doing nails with McKenna when I was 8

Gymnastics is my <u>most</u> favorite thing in the whole world. My best friend, Katie, and I have gone to the same gym since we were six years old. But it doesn't have a competitive team, so McKenna invited me to Aberg's Gymnastics, where she coaches.

McKenna Brooks coaches the Xcel Silver and Gold teams at Aberg's Gymnastics. She is a senior in college working toward her degree in elementary education.

I thought I would join the Xcel Silver team, but McKenna thinks I'm ready for Gold. The Gold skills are TOUGH, though. Here's what I'm working on:

FLOOR
Roundoff back handspring

BARS
- Squat on low bar and jump to high bar (YES to the squat. YIKES to the jump!)
- Dismount from high bar (But how can I dismount if I never mount?)

VAULT
Roundoff or front handspring (We practice with a real vault table and land in a squishy foam pit. It's kind of scary but so fun!)

BEAM
Cartwheel (so easy on the floor but so hard on the beam!)

McKenna says if I get some of these skills by the end of summer, I can compete on Gold. Otherwise I'll bump back down to Silver. Summer ends in less than a month (gulp), but McKenna believes in me. So I'm going to devote ALL my time to gymnastics. I've got like 30 days to get some Gold skills and make McKenna proud!

It's hard to do gymnastics without my best friend, though. Whenever I'm at the new gym, I REALLY miss Katie. Here we are at our old gym:

I did our hair!

MY 5 FAVORITE THINGS ABOUT KATIE GUNDERSEN:

1. She can make even boring things more fun.
2. She likes twinning and lets me do her hair however I want.
3. She LOVES our traditions, like French-braid Fridays, pancakes after sleepovers, and trick-or-treating together. When Katie got sick and couldn't go with me last Halloween, she had a total meltdown because we broke our tradition!

4. We grew up together on the same street in St. Paul, Minnesota.
5. She's been my best friend for 10¼ years (my whole life).

LOL! Katie just called. It's like she KNEW I was journaling about her. When I read her what I wrote, she said to write this:

KATIE'S 5 FAVORITE THINGS ABOUT ME:

1. Lila is my best friend on the entire planet. She's more than a bestie. She's pretty much my sister.

2. Lila always knows how to make me feel better, like when I had a meltdown last Halloween. But I can't believe you told everyone about that, Lila!!! (Gulp. Sorry, Katie.)
3. Lila is like a celebrity hairstylist. Seriously.
4. Lila is super bendy. (She means I'm flexible, like I can do the front splits and side splits.)

5. Lila never changes—except her hair—and I know I can always count on her. (Aw)

THURSDAY, AUGUST 8

Here's a photo of my new teammates. I wish Katie was with me, standing right by my side.

McKenna

Me

Avery

Emilia

At my old gym, Katie and I talked and laughed during warm-ups. But things are more serious on the Xcel team—at least with Avery. Emilia can be funny sometimes. Whenever we practice tough skills, she's like, "I'm freaking out. Are you freaking out? Because I'm freaking out." But Avery is all business. She's been on Gold for a year already, so she keeps telling me what to do.

This is pretty much how practice tonight went:

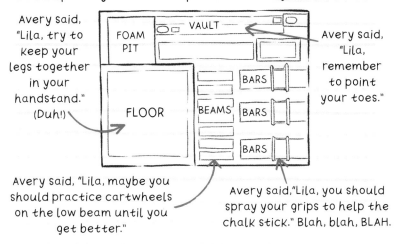

Avery said, "Lila, try to keep your legs together in your handstand." (Duh!)

Avery said, "Lila, remember to point your toes."

Avery said, "Lila, maybe you should practice cartwheels on the low beam until you get better."

Avery said, "Lila, you should spray your grips to help the chalk stick." Blah, blah, BLAH.

When Avery found out McKenna used to be my babysitter, Avery asked, "Is that why you think you'll get on the Gold team?" She said it like she doesn't think I'm good enough to earn a spot on Gold on my own!!!

McKenna knows I miss my old gym. She grew up in Seattle, and she told me she missed her old gym when she came to Minneapolis. But she made new friends, and she says I will too.

I hope McKenna is right. I'm nervous about my new teammates judging me. I wish Katie would join Aberg's too! She isn't sure she wants to try competitive gymnastics, so she's sticking with our old gym. ☹

Dad picked me up from practice tonight. Aberg's is in Minneapolis, and we live in St. Paul. Minneapolis and St. Paul are called the "Twin Cities" because they're so close together.

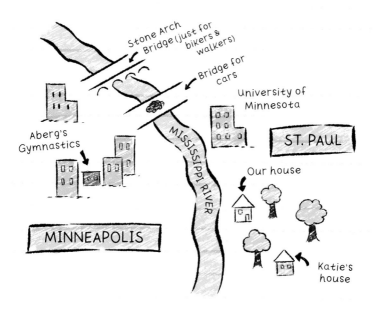

A lot of the buildings around Aberg's are shiny and new, but the houses in our neighborhood are about a hundred years old. I love our old house, even if there's always something that needs fixing. Luckily, Dad is really handy. Mom says he would be bored if there wasn't something to repair, repaint, or replace.

Dad will NEVER run out of work to do on our house!

Jack's my 8-year-old brother.

Mom's wearing scrubs because she's a nurse at the children's hospital.

On the way home, Dad asked how practice went. He's a psychologist, so he's a really good listener. I told him about Emilia and Avery and about how much I missed Katie. Dad said, "Give it some time. Try to get to know your teammates for who they are. They won't replace Katie—"

"NO ONE can replace Katie," I interrupted.

Dad nodded. "But Emilia and Avery could become new friends, right?"

I said "right," but I wasn't so sure.

LITTLE BROTHER ALERT!

Jack's supposed to knock before he comes into my room, but he NEVER does. Whenever he barges in, I say, "Jack! Knock!" He just says, "Who's there?"

Tonight he busted in to tell me all about the horse camp he's going to on Monday with his buddy Marshall. Jack talked nonstop, and then suddenly got quiet. I asked if he was "ner-cited." That's Dad's word for when your stomach flip-flops and you can't tell what you feel. Jack gets nervous when he goes to new places, so I remind him that he's ALSO excited. I asked what he was most excited about, and he said meeting the horses and other animals.

When he was feeling better, I tried to braid his hair, which made him run away. Jack hates it when people mess with his hair, so that's my best big sister trick for getting alone time.

My plan for Jack's hair

Then I thought about gymnastics, and I felt ner-cited too. I'm SUPER excited about learning new skills and competing in meets. But here's what I'm nervous about:

1. Will I get enough new skills to make the Gold team in less than a month?
2. Will I be good enough to compete in meets and make McKenna proud?
3. Will I make new friends at my new gym?

FRIDAY, AUGUST 9

Mom just told us that Jack's friend Marshall broke his arm and can't go to horse camp. Jack is so disappointed. When Mom asked if I wanted to take Marshall's place and go with Jack, I didn't know what to say. I mean, it would be fun to learn how to ride a horse. And it's not sleep-away camp, so I would be home at night to work on gymnastics. But I NEED to master the Gold skills, and I don't have that much time.

I texted Katie right away, and she wrote back "I want to go too!!!" Katie LOVES animals (especially baby animals). But when her mom checked online, camp was full. ☹ So now we're hanging out at our favorite park and Katie is helping me list the pros and cons of going to camp. (We learned how to do this at school last year to help us make decisions.)

 **PROS**  **CONS**

I'll learn how to ride a horse.	I may be too tired to practice gymnastics when I get home at night.
Jack will have a buddy at camp.	*It's another thing you'd be doing without your best friend.*
It'll be an adventure!	*You might fall off a horse and get hurt.*
You might get to braid some horse hair. (Katie wrote that!)	*You won't be able to do gymnastics if you're hurt!*

When Katie kind of took over the cons list, I said maybe we should just do some gymnastics instead. I get that Katie doesn't want me to go to horse camp without her. But what do I want?

SATURDAY, AUGUST 10

So I woke up STILL not knowing what to do about horse camp. Then I went to gymnastics, where I forgot all about horses for a while. McKenna started practice like she always does. She asks: "Ready to work?" And we all say READY TO FLY

During stretching, we played a get-to-know-your-teammates game. I found out that Emilia broke her ankle last year at gymnastics. Is that why she worries so much when we try tough skills? I learned that Avery is the oldest of FIVE kids. Maybe that's why she's always telling me what to do! Like today, she told me all the things I could get points taken off for when I compete in meets.

Lila, you're not holding your hands the right way.

Lila, don't fall off the bars or you'll lose half a point!

Lila, you have to stick your landing!

McKenna reminded Avery that I have a coach—I don't need two. But it was too late. I was already nervous about jumping to the high bar. And when someone tells you NOT to fall off, all you can think about is falling off!

I tried to do a squat-on landing, with both feet on the low bar. That's the first step to jumping to the high bar. But I only got one foot up in my squat. Emilia said I'd better not catch my other toe on the low bar, or I could fall forward and break my arm. REALLY??? Why would she say that while I was on the bars?

This is what I was trying to do

McKenna said not to worry—that's why she teaches us how to fall forward. You're supposed to do a flip so you land safely on your back on the mat. But I don't want to learn how to FALL. I want to learn how to jump to the high bar!

The good part of practice was when I told McKenna about horse camp. She said she used to volunteer at a horseback riding center when she was my age! She also said riding is good training for gymnastics because it helps your legs and core (a bunch of muscles in your stomach, back, and hips) get stronger.

McKenna and I came up with ways I could work on gymnastics at camp, like . . .

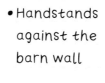

- Handstands against the barn wall

- Sprinting along the fence (the horses might run with me!)

- Tumbling in the grass

- Cartwheels on top of the fence, like a beam (Just kidding! McKenna made me promise NOT to try that.)

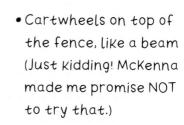

By the time I got home, I'd made my decision. I'm going to horse camp! For two weeks. Where I'll have fun _and_ work on my gymnastics.

But camp starts in only 2 days. What do I need for camp???

Okay, this is what the camp website says I should bring:

 HONEYCRISP DAY CAMP PACKING LIST

☐ Long pants

☐ Boots with a smooth sole and raised heel

☐ Riding helmet ← (Mom says we can rent these at camp.)

☐ Water bottle and sack lunch

☐ Sunscreen

☐ Instant camera! Phones aren't allowed, but I want to take pictures for Katie so she'll feel like she's at camp with me.

Check out the riding boots Mom is getting for me. SO cute!

MONDAY, AUGUST 12

Welcome to Honeycrisp Hill Horse Camp! (Dad says Honeycrisp apples were invented right here in Minnesota.)

At camp, we were divided into groups named after kinds of horses. Jack and I are both in the Palomino group. And guess who else is in our group?

Yep, that's Emilia. She's my teammate at the gym AND at camp.

Emilia's friend Jade

Mr. Benson owns the camp. He took us on a hayride!

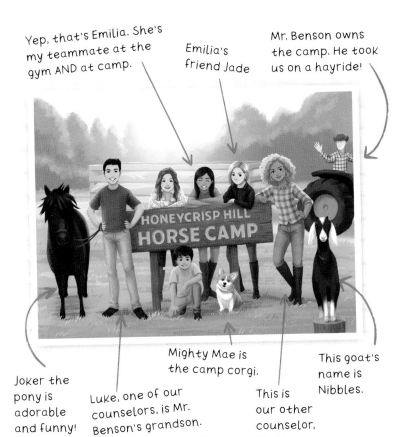

Joker the pony is adorable and funny!

Luke, one of our counselors, is Mr. Benson's grandson.

Mighty Mae is the camp corgi.

This is our other counselor, Freya.

This goat's name is Nibbles.

This is what we saw on our hayride:

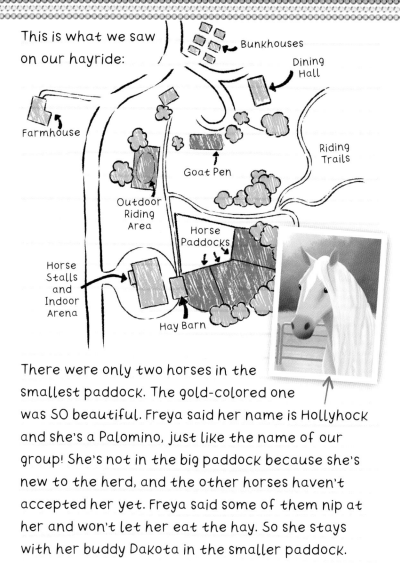

Bunkhouses

Dining Hall

Farmhouse

Riding Trails

Goat Pen

Outdoor Riding Area

Horse Paddocks

Horse Stalls and Indoor Arena

Hay Barn

There were only two horses in the smallest paddock. The gold-colored one was SO beautiful. Freya said her name is Hollyhock and she's a Palomino, just like the name of our group! She's not in the big paddock because she's new to the herd, and the other horses haven't accepted her yet. Freya said some of them nip at her and won't let her eat the hay. So she stays with her buddy Dakota in the smaller paddock.

Well, I know all about being the new girl. It's just like me at my new gym! No wonder I was drawn to Hollyhock right away. She and I have a lot in common.

When we got our schedule for the day, I was SO pumped. We were going to ride horses next! I hoped I'd get to ride Hollyhock.

PALOMINOS
Monday Schedule

9:00 – Hayride/Tour
10:00 – Riding
11:00 – Grooming
12:00 – Lunch
1:00 – Free Time
2:00 – Arts & Crafts
3:00 – Prep for Pickup

When we went into the barn lounge to try on helmets, I looked through the window into the arena. I saw four horses, but Hollyhock wasn't one of them. ☹

Freya and Luke told us about the horses: BEN is a very mellow quarter horse. Freya said he's 22 years old, which is about 65 in human years!

JOKER is a ~~mischeivous~~ mischievous pony with a very shaggy mane.

20

DAKOTA is a super chill paint horse. (Jack said, "Whoa, that horse can PAINT?" Luke laughed and said "paint" refers to her black and white coat.)

CINNAMON is a sassy chestnut. She is full of energy and good for riders who want to go, go, go!

I wanted to ride Dakota because she shares a pen with Hollyhock. But Jade chose her first. So I chose Cinnamon. Emilia was all like, "Be careful on that sassy horse!" But I wasn't worried. I was excited!

Emilia chose old Ben, and Jack went right for Joker, the mischievous pony. I was proud of my little brother. When it comes to horses, he seems a lot more excited than nervous.

Luke and Freya said we would get to know all the horses really well, and that we could ride our favorites on Parents Day, the last day of camp. We're going to do a big riding demo to show off our skills for our parents. I hope I'll have some skills to show off by then!

Before we got on our horses, Luke taught us how to greet them. Horses' eyes are on the sides of their heads, so you should approach them from the side and make sure they see you. Then let the horse sniff your hand. It'll smell you and blow a puff of warm air on your hand. Cinnamon said hi to me this way!

1. STARTING: Squeeze your legs against your horse's sides. That means "start walking."

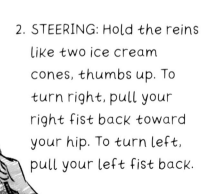

2. STEERING: Hold the reins like two ice cream cones, thumbs up. To turn right, pull your right fist back toward your hip. To turn left, pull your left fist back.

Joker doesn't seem to care about space. He stops to play with a cone whenever he wants!

3. SPACING: Don't follow too closely behind the horse in front of you. Luke said to look between your horse's ears and make sure you can see the hooves of the horse in front of you.

4. STOPPING: Sink into the saddle and blow out your breath while pulling back on the reins.

That's a LOT to remember. But when Freya found out that Emilia and I do gymnastics, she said gymnasts make good riders. I think she's right. I felt strong in the saddle, like I could ride all day!

When it was time for grooming, I got the best surprise. We went into this big grooming stall, and Hollyhock was there! She was even more beautiful up close.

I held out my hand for her to sniff, and she blew her warm breath on me. Hollyhock smelled like sweet hay and golden sunshine. I think I fell in love with her at first sniff!

Freya said not to stand right behind Hollyhock when we brush her tail. And if we need to walk behind her, we should put our hand on her rump so she knows where we are and doesn't spook. Freya said a spooked horse might kick.

I love the blaze on Hollyhoock's forehead

Look at these sweet white stockings

When Emilia heard that, she took a huge step away from Hollyhock's rump. But I stepped toward it, with my hand on her back. I couldn't wait to braid her long, beautiful white tail!

Jack and I stood on one side of Hollyhock, and Emilia and Jade stood on the other. We groomed her with special combs and brushes. I used a soft brush to make Hollyhock's coat shiny. I think she liked it because she kind of closed her eyes and leaned into me. It felt like a horse hug, and I hugged her right back.

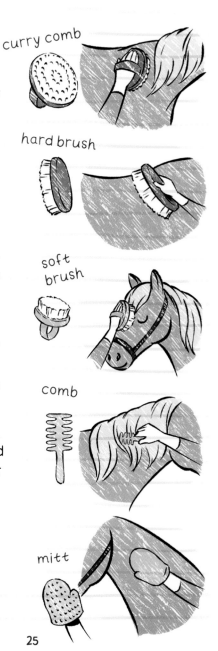

curry comb

hard brush

soft brush

comb

mitt

I tried to be extra gentle when I combed out the snarls in Hollyhock's tail. But horse hair is a LOT thicker and coarser than human hair. When her tail finally felt smooth, I gave her a French braid. It looked so pretty! Freya let Emilia and Jade add some colored extensions and gems to her mane. I added some wildflowers to her tail and did my own hair to match.

Like Katie says, we're twinning!

I was so busy grooming Hollyhock, I didn't notice that Jack was gone. But then I spotted him. Jack found the goat! Now I know why he's named Nibbles.

Jack looked really happy. He'd already found his buddies at camp.

I didn't have any buddies at camp yet. But then I leaned toward Hollyhock and breathed in her sweet horsey smell, and I decided SHE would be my buddy.

I asked Freya when I could ride Hollyhock, but she said only the counselors are riding her because she spooked easily when she first got to camp. Freya said Hollyhock might be ready to ride later this week or next week, but she would need a confident rider.

Right then and there, I made a decision. I am going to prove to the counselors that I'm a good rider—a confident rider. I want to be the one to ride Hollyhock first. Maybe even for Parents Day!

TUESDAY, AUGUST 13

I couldn't wait to get back to camp and start riding. When Mom dropped us off, Mighty Mae barked and raced around Jack's legs. Luke said she was "herding" Jack.

"She's not hurting me," Jack said.

"Herding," Luke said. "H-E-R-D-I-N-G. She's making sure you don't wander away!"

Mighty Mae loves playing tug-of-war!

When it was time to ride, Emilia chose Ben again, but Freya said we should get to know different horses. Emilia sighed, but then she got on Dakota and I got on Ben.

Riding Ben felt SO different from riding Cinnamon. Ben didn't seem to want to go. I had to squeeze my legs hard just to get him to walk—and then suddenly he started to TROT!

I felt pretty good about getting old Ben moving. I want to prove I can ride any horse, even the slow ones. Then maybe I'll get to ride Hollyhock!

Oops! Peanut butter smudge. I'm writing this during lunch.

TUESDAY AFTERNOON

This afternoon, we got to ride in the outdoor ring! Freya said Joker would need a strong rider, because he loves to eat grass when he's not supposed to. I raised my hand right away. I wanted to prove that I was a strong rider.

But whoa, was that pony naughty! He kept trying to sneak a mouthful of grass. He wandered into the middle of the ring a couple of times too. Then Freya gave me a good steering tip. She told me to look where I want to go, because my body will shift that way and tell Joker where I want to go. Cool, right?

I must have done pretty well with Joker, because while we were learning how to draw horses in arts and crafts, Luke pulled me aside. He said I could try riding Hollyhock tomorrow!!! He thinks we will be a good match. I just about fell out of my chair, I was so excited.

Emilia overheard and said, "Are you sure you want to be the first one to ride a new horse? What if she bucks? What if she starts running and you fall off?"

But I was sure. I've never been more sure of anything in my whole entire life. I'm going to ride Hollyhock tomorrow!

This is how I'll groom Hollyhock if I get to ride her on Parents Day—I mean, <u>when</u> I get to ride her on Parents Day. A girl has to think positive, right?

TUESDAY NIGHT (SIGH)

Well, gymnastics started out okay. When McKenna asked if we were ready to work, I shouted, "Ready to fly!" Because after learning I could ride Hollyhock tomorrow, I felt ready to fly straight up to that high bar.

I tuned out all the noise and distraction in the gym. I squatted on the low bar with both feet. I took a deep breath, and I flew forward.

I grabbed the high bar with both hands, and my feet swung out in front of me. But my fingers slipped! And then I was falling.

I landed flat on my back with a thud. I couldn't breathe. My brain said, "You're okay. Just breathe." But I couldn't!

Emilia leaned over me. She looked so worried that I thought maybe I had hurt myself. But finally, I could breathe again.

McKenna said I should take a break, but I didn't want her to think I was scared. So I tried to get back on the bars. But my body wasn't working!

I told McKenna I needed new grips (which is kind of true), so I sat out and stretched until we moved to beam.

I missed Katie SO much right then. She would have found a way to make me feel better. But when I got home and texted her, she was hanging out with a friend from our old gym (ouch).

My palms are still sweating. What's wrong with me? How do I make it stop?

THIS WAS ME:

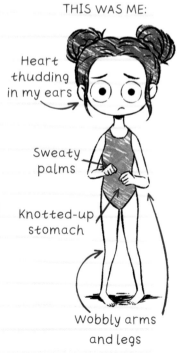

Heart thudding in my ears

Sweaty palms

Knotted-up stomach

Wobbly arms and legs

I couldn't sleep AT ALL last night. Well, I must have slept a little, because I had nightmares. I kept dreaming about falling off the high bar, and then right before hitting the mats, I'd wake up.

The early morning nightmares were the worst part of my day. But riding Hollyhock? That was like the <u>best</u> dream ever.

When Luke led her into the indoor arena, I felt like I had just won a gold medal.

Hollyhock remembered me from Monday—I know she did! She nickered and lowered her head toward me. And she stood perfectly still while Luke helped me mount her.

As soon as I got in the saddle, I reached down and gave Hollyhock lots of pats. While Luke talked about what we were going to do today, her ears pricked forward, like she was listening. Like she wanted to do a good job!

Jack's photo bomb

We walked around the arena twice, and then we trotted. Hollyhock trotted for me right away. I think she wanted to be ridden just as much as I wanted to ride her. She was such a good girl!

Luke was right—Hollyhock and I ARE a good match. I felt so proud being the first camper to ride her. And since it went well, I'm pretty sure I'll get to ride her for Parents Day. I can't wait!

THURSDAY, AUGUST 15

I rode Hollyhock in the morning, and I knew Emilia
was a little jealous because she kept staring at
me. So at the start of the afternoon ride, she
asked right away if she could ride Hollyhock.

I couldn't breathe for a second. I'd only been riding
Hollyhock for a day, but somehow it already felt
like she was my special horse. I wasn't ready to
share her! But Luke and Freya say we have to take
turns with the horses, so I had to pretend it didn't
bother me as I climbed on old Ben and Emilia
mounted Hollyhock.

Then here's what happened:
1. Emilia let Hollyhock get
   way too close to
   Cinnamon.

2. Cinnamon turned
   around and nipped
   at Hollyhock!

3. Hollyhock startled and
   stepped sideways.

Freya reminded Emilia that the other horses don't know Hollyhock well, so they might nip or kick at her if she gets too close. She told Emilia to hold Hollyhock back and be careful about spacing. But Emilia was really freaked out and wanted to switch horses.

That was my big chance! I said I would switch with her. But as Emilia walked past me, she warned me again to be careful on Hollyhock. "I practically fell off!" she said.

For a second, I thought about my fall from the high bar. But as soon as I swung into the saddle, I knew I wouldn't fall off Hollyhock.

BACK OFF!
YOU'RE TOO
CLOSE!

I rode Hollyhock around the ring and gave her lots of pats and reassurance. I made sure she didn't get too close to the other horses. I was NOT going to let her get nipped again.

While I was riding Hollyhock, I pretended it was Parents Day. Then I pretended we weren't at Honeycrisp Hill at all. I imagined Hollyhock was my very own horse, and we were galloping off into the sunset . . .

Luke brought me back to Earth when he told us what we get to do tomorrow—a trail ride! I wished I could fast-forward to the trail ride, like zooming through a video to get to the good part. Then I remembered what I had to do between now and then.

GYMNASTICS.

I suddenly had butterflies in my stomach, which didn't make any sense. I've been doing gymnastics for as long as I can remember! Jumping to the high bar is new, but learning a new skill has never worried me like this before. And I CAN'T freak out—I only have a few weeks to learn some Gold skills!

That's when I thought of the skills McKenna gave me to work on at camp. So during free time, I joined Jack, Nibbles, and Mighty Mae in the field. Here's what I did:

- Push-ups (Nibbles joined in and tried to climb on my back!)
- Handstands against the fence
- Cartwheels on top of the fence (Just kidding!) But I did find a log to use as a beam.
- Running up and down the hill by the barn

Afterward, I was still nervous about going back to the gym, but it felt great to run and tumble. It was the first time I ever did a balance beam routine with a goat!

THURSDAY NIGHT

I tried. I REALLY tried. I packed my new grips. I wore my favorite leo. I even added colored extensions and sparkly hair gems to my braids, just like the ones Freya let us use with Hollyhock. Fun hairdos always give me confidence.

Favorite Leotard

Emilia said she liked my hair, but Avery gave me a weird look. She asked if I'd dyed my hair. When I said I was wearing extensions, she said, "But why?" It felt like a nip—like how Cinnamon nipped Hollyhock. So I decided to work on spacing, not getting too close to Avery. (I figured if it works for horses, it might work for humans too.)

I chose the beam farthest away from Avery. I was trying to get my cartwheel, and McKenna said I should look at the beam where I'm about to land. That sounded like what Freya told me at camp—to look where you want to go when you ride a horse.

So I tried McKenna's tip. I wobbled at the end
of my cartwheel, but it was the best one I've
done yet. So maybe horse camp IS helping my
gymnastics.

When we moved to bars, Avery pointed
out that I was getting hair gems everywhere.
I mean, some of them did fall off (one was
stuck to the bottom of my foot). But
so what? Avery got <u>chalk</u> everywhere!
So I ignored her.

I was ready to forget my fall on the bars and try
again. I put on my new grips and mounted the low
bar, easy peasy. When it was time to jump to
the high bar, I told myself, "You can do this!"

But somehow . . . I just . . . couldn't. My body
wouldn't move! I felt frozen, like an ice sculpture.
All I could do was slide backward off the low bar.
WHAT'S WRONG WITH ME???

Avery came over and said that it took her a while to jump to the high bar too. I thought she was going to be nice for a change. Then she said, "But you need to jump to the high bar to be on the Gold team. Maybe you should stick with Silver."

I kept hearing Avery's voice in my head, even when we moved to vault. As I sprinted down the runway, that voice got so loud, it messed me up. Instead of springing over the vault table, I flopped onto it.

Emilia gasped, like it was the worst wipeout she'd ever seen. Where was Katie when I needed her??? She would have cracked a joke and made me laugh.

Lila, are you okay?

When McKenna asked if I was okay, I fibbed and said yes. I can't disappoint McKenna—she believes in me. She thinks I'm ready for Gold! But am I? I just don't know anymore.

I texted Katie on the way home. I may not have a buddy at the gym, but my best friend is still there when I need her. We're going to meet at the park.

THURSDAY NIGHT (STILL)

Katie ~~always~~ usually makes me feel better. But tonight, well . . . here's what happened.

I told her about feeling frozen on the bars and about what Avery said about sticking with the Silver team. Then I asked, "What if Avery is right? What if I'm not cut out for Gold?"

I expected Katie to be all, "Lila Maria Monetti, don't say that. You've GOT this." But instead, she said, "You can come back to our old gym!" Her eyes got all hopeful, like she wanted me to fail so that I'd have to quit the team. What kind of a best friend is that???

So now I can't sleep. And I HAVE to sleep so I'll be ready to ride Hollyhock on the trail tomorrow. Maybe I can count horses instead of sheep. Is that a thing?

FRIDAY, AUGUST 16

In the morning, as I pulled on my riding boots, I was SO excited about my trail ride with Hollyhock. At first, Hollyhock was such a good girl. She followed her buddy Dakota onto the trail.

HILLY PART OF TRAIL

Mr. Benson said to lean back going downhill and forward going up. Going downhill felt scary—like I was going to slide forward right out of the saddle. My palms started sweating, just like on the bars at the gym!

DISASTER ZONE

Then disaster struck. A squirrel scampered out of a bush. A dog burst out behind it. Hollyhock spooked and jumped sideways. And I FELL OFF!!!

Right before I hit the ground, I rolled like I learned in gymnastics and landed on my shoulder. When I sat up, Mr. Benson was rushing toward Hollyhock to grab her reins. She looked SO scared—her nostrils quivered and her ears flicked back and forth.

I wanted to comfort her, but when Freya helped me up, my legs wobbled. Mr. Benson got on Hollyhock and said I should ride Dakota instead. He said, "Maybe Hollyhock isn't ready to be ridden after all."

My chest got tight and I blurted, "It's not her fault! Why was that dog running loose?" Mr. Benson said lots of farm dogs run loose in the area. The other horses are used to them, but Hollyhock isn't.

Why can't farmers keep better track of their dogs? Poor Hollyhock!

On the ride back, Emilia kept asking me if I was okay. She said, "I knew that horse was going to spook!"

Then Emilia said she'd heard about another camp horse named Snowball who kept spooking, and he had to be sold to a new owner.

After I heard that, I couldn't get back to the barn fast enough. I found Mr. Benson and asked him if Hollyhock would get sent away like Snowball. He said that it was too soon to tell—that not all horses make good camp horses.

"But she IS a good horse!" I said. "She's sweet and gentle and the most beautiful horse ever."

Mr. Benson was quiet for a long moment. Then he said he was going to work with Hollyhock to make her more spook-proof around dogs. But he couldn't make any promises. For now, he said, she can't be ridden by campers. She can only be ridden by experienced riders.

"I _am_ an experienced rider!" I wanted to say. Except I couldn't, because I'd just fallen off Hollyhock. Maybe a more experienced rider would have kept her calm. Maybe a more experienced rider wouldn't have fallen off!

So now it's free time, and a bunch of other "maybes" are racing through my mind like dogs across the trail.

Maybe I pushed to ride Hollyhock before I was a good enough rider.

Maybe she IS going to get sent away, and it's all my fault!!!

Maybe I wasn't ready.

Maybe Hollyhock wasn't ready.

Maybe I ruined her chances of being a camp horse.

I got to see Hollyhock one more time before Dad picked us up. I went to her pen, and she came right up, close enough for me to smell her sweet scent. She nuzzled me with her velvety nose, and I wrapped my arms around her neck and gave her the biggest hug. I told her it wasn't her fault. I told her how sorry I was.

When I stroked her head under her forelock, she closed her eyes a little. She trusts me SO much—I know she does. She thinks we'll get to ride together on Monday. But I know that I won't get to ride her on Monday.

I won't get to ride her on Parents Day. I might not ever get to ride my sweet, beautiful horse again.

SATURDAY, AUGUST 17

I don't want to go to gymnastics this morning.
My phone keeps buzzing, and I know it's Katie,
but I don't want to talk to her. If I tell her
what happened on the trail ride, she'll probably
say, "Now you can quit camp and just hang out
with me!"

I want to stay in bed and pull the covers over my
head, blocking out the whole entire world. But
when I don't get up in time, Dad sends Jack in. My
brother is already creeping toward my bed. He
thinks he's going to scare me, but I'm ready.

I started tickling Jack through my covers. Then he
saw the ginormous bruise on my shoulder. He asked
if it hurt, and it does a little. But not nearly as
much as my heart hurts every time I think about
Hollyhock.

I did go to gymnastics, but I couldn't stop thinking about Hollyhock. Emilia said, "Wow, look at your shoulder!" Then she told everyone what happened at camp.

McKenna said I could sit out anything that hurt my shoulder. The old me would have said, "I'm okay. I'm ready to fly!" But I'm NOT ready to fly. I'm not sure I'm ready for anything anymore, so all I could do was shrug (which did kind of hurt).

While Avery was practicing her floor routine, McKenna pulled out her phone to show me parts of a Gold routine that she's creating for ME. "Start thinking about music, okay?" she said, as if I was already on the Gold team.

I wanted to shout, "Whoa! I don't know if I'm good enough for Gold!"

That's when Avery took a nip at me. And this time, I nipped right back

You know that if your shoulder doesn't heal in time, you won't be able to compete on Gold, right?

AVERY

You know what, Avery? It doesn't help me when you say stuff like that. Are you trying to freak me out?

ME

If you can't say anything nice, don't talk to me AT ALL.

ME AGAIN

McKenna hurried over and said it was time to regroup. We played a team game on beam where we had to take turns doing leaps. Our goal was to do ten leaps without falling, and we were supposed to cheer each other on. Avery barely said a word.

When Emilia said my split leaps were really good, I felt better. But I'm starting to worry if I'm actually ready for the Gold team.

SUNDAY, AUGUST 18

I'm lying in bed, trying to remember my dream. I was at the gym watching Hollyhock on the beam. (Dreams are so weird!) She

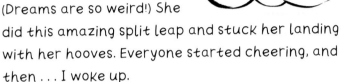

did this amazing split leap and stuck her landing with her hooves. Everyone started cheering, and then . . . I woke up.

SHOOT! I hate it when good dreams end. But the dream got me thinking about how I can help Hollyhock. If Mr. Benson is going to train her, can I cheer her on somehow?

When Katie texted, I texted right back. I told her what happened on the trail ride Friday and how I needed to help my favorite horse. I hoped Katie would help me come up with ways to cheer on Hollyhock. But instead . . .

YOU FELL OFF A HORSE TWO DAYS AGO AND DIDN'T TELL ME???

KATIE

I'm sorry. I wanted to tell you.
ME

You have this whole new life this summer and you don't tell me anything anymore.
KATIE

But it seems like you don't want to hear about horse camp or gymnastics.
ME

Sometimes I think you just want me to quit so that everything will go back to how it used to be.
ME

···
KATIE

I could tell Katie was writing something because three dots kept bouncing on the screen. But when they disappeared and she didn't text back, I felt totally alone. Just like at gymnastics.

MONDAY, AUGUST 19

Usually Jack is the first one out of Mom's car in the morning. He's so confident at camp that he runs off to find Luke and doesn't even wait for me. But today I jumped out of the car first and ran straight to the barn to find Mr. Benson.

He was unloading hay bales from a wagon. Right away, I asked if I could help him train Hollyhock. I said I felt like it was my fault that she might get sent away.

Mr. Benson stroked his beard for a long time, but he finally smiled. He said if I met him in the arena during free time, he knew of a way I could help. YES!

When it was training time, Mighty Mae and I went to work. Here's what we did:
- I stood in the middle of the arena holding Mighty Mae's leash.
- Mr. Benson used a lead rope to walk Hollyhock around us in a big circle.
- Mr. Benson talked to her in a calm voice and gave her lots of pats and horse treats.

- Then we traded places. Mr. Benson and Hollyhock stood in the middle and Mae and I walked around them.

Hollyhock kept an eye on Mighty Mae at ALL times. Her ears swiveled like she was keeping an ear out for danger too. Whenever we got too close, Hollyhock's eyes widened and her nostrils started quivering. But Mr. Benson kept reassuring her.

After a little while (and a lot of horse treats), Hollyhock let us walk around her without acting scared. I was so proud of her!

The only hard part was leaving her in her paddock afterward. We led her in, and then we led Dakota out for the afternoon riding session. When we left Hollyhock alone, she whinnied and ran along the fence, like she wanted to come too. But she couldn't. Not yet.

Mr. Benson said we can do more training during free time this week. I'm crossing my fingers that it will work. It has to work!

TUESDAY, AUGUST 20

Today during training, Mr. Benson had me walk with
Mighty Mae toward Hollyhock. She let us take only
a few steps before she snorted and pinned back
her ears. But Mr. Benson kept saying, "It's okay, girl.
You're not in danger. You're okay."

He told me to talk to her in a calm voice too. "If
you act nervous, she'll feel more nervous," he said.
"But if you act calm, she'll calm down too." So as I
took another step toward Hollyhock, I told her
what a good, brave girl she was.

She didn't let us get super close,
but I was still proud of her! I got to
give her a treat—a little orange
nugget made of carrots and oats.
She chomped it up like it was the
most delicious cookie in the world.

Afterward, I found the rest of my team
cleaning stalls. Sometimes we help scoop
"horse apples," a fancy
name for horse poop. But
Jack was pushing a load of
a different kind.

Nibbles loves riding
in the wheelbarrow!

56

When Emilia asked me what I'd been doing, I told her.

You're so brave.
If I'd fallen off Hollyhock like you did, I'd be too nervous to be in the ring with her!

EMILIA

Well, I am kind of nervous, but I can't let Hollyhock know that. Mr. Benson says you have to act calm and confident around horses, even when you don't feel it.

ME

Yeah, I can't do that. When I'm nervous, EVERYONE knows it. All my worries spill out! But it helps me to talk about them, like at gymnastics.

EMILIA

When Emilia said that, it got me thinking. Maybe my new teammate isn't trying to be dramatic. Maybe she just gets nervous, and talking about her worries is how she makes herself feel better.

Talking to Katie is what used to make me feel better. But I haven't talked to my best friend in two whole days. (sigh) So I'm going to have to figure out a new way to make myself feel better at gymnastics.

Wow. So much happened at practice tonight!

FIRST

Avery said she was sorry for making me feel bad on Saturday. She said she was only trying to help me get better.

I could tell by the look on her face that she really was sorry. So I thought about how I'm trying to help Hollyhock get better, and I said,

It doesn't help me when you tell me what I'm doing wrong. But maybe you could tell me what I'm doing right.

Avery nodded and said, "I'll try."

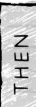

THEN

Emilia told Avery how brave I was for helping train a horse at camp, and how she wished she were as brave as me. She was kind of going overboard, so I blurted out that I wasn't always brave—that I get scared too.

THEN...

Avery said, "You mean like on the bars?"

I felt like I was standing in a bright spotlight! I thought about making some excuse or trying to change the subject. But I'd been hiding my fear at the gym for nearly two weeks now, and it hadn't gotten me anywhere. I finally told Avery the truth.

I admitted that the bars totally freaked me out and that I didn't know if I'd ever be able to jump to the high bar and that I probably should just stick with the Silver team. It all came out in a rush.

 THEN...

I realized McKenna was standing right behind me! (gulp)

When McKenna pulled me aside, I spilled the beans about everything—that I was scared I might not be ready for Gold and would let McKenna down, and scared I'd lost my best friend, and scared that my sweet horse Hollyhock might get sent away because I rode her before she was ready. Then I got this huge lump in my throat.

McKenna gave me a hug. Then she pulled up an image on her phone of a green leafy plant. It turns out hollyhock is a kind of plant! But it looked so plain. Why was such a pretty horse named for such a boring plant?

Then McKenna showed me another hollyhock covered in pink flowers. She said her grandma used to plant hollyhocks in Seattle and that they didn't bloom until their second year. "They bloomed when they were ready," McKenna said. "And so will you."

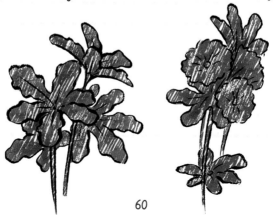

McKenna said lots of other reassuring things, like . . .

- I'm a Gold gymnast in training. No one masters a skill the first time they try it. Falling and failing are part of training.
- I can take a step back on bars if I need to. Sometimes you have to go back to the last skill you felt confident doing, and start from there.
- I could take a step back to the Silver team if I need to. (Ouch. I really, REALLY hope I don't need to!)
- With enough time and practice, I'll get where I want to be. I'll bloom when I'm ready, just like a hollyhock.
- Sometimes friends need to take a step away too. But best friends find their way back to each other.

Maybe McKenna's right, but will there be enough time? There are only three days left of camp—and school starts in two weeks! I might not make the Gold team. I might have to bump back to Silver. But I hope, hope, hope there's enough time to help get Hollyhock back on track.

WEDNESDAY, AUGUST 21

Today during training, I walked Mighty Mae slowly toward Hollyhock. This time, Hollyhock didn't look spooked. She looked curious. She stretched her neck toward us and pricked her ears forward.

When Mighty Mae and I took another step, Hollyhock started chewing, like she had something in her mouth. Mr. Benson said that meant she was super focused on the little dog in front of her.

I took the last step v-e-r-y slowly because I didn't want to spook Hollyhock. I told her what a good, brave girl she was. And then . . .

Hollyhock took a step toward us! She lowered her head and blew out a puff of warm air. She sniffed in Mighty Mae's direction, and Mae sniffed right back. My two favorite animals were nose to nose!

I gave Hollyhock a treat for being so brave, and Mr. Benson said I deserved one too. I thought he meant the crunchy orange carrot-oat thingies (gross!). But he said I'd earned the right to ride Hollyhock again.

YESSS!!!

My stomach fluttered, but I had to act confident for Hollyhock. I had to show her that I believed in her and trusted her. So I took a big breath and got back on the horse.

While we rode around the arena, I kept my voice calm and gave Hollyhock lots of gentle pats and encouragement. She stayed calm too. She paid attention to my steering cues and even trotted when I gave her a gentle squeeze with my legs. She was SUCH a good girl!

It wasn't exactly a trail ride, I know. But sometimes you have to take a step backward to move forward, just like in gymnastics.

THURSDAY, AUGUST 22

Today, three exciting things happened:

1. Freya let me ride Hollyhock during the regular riding session—with other horses in the ring!

2. During free time, I helped Mr. Benson train Hollyhock in the outdoor ring. He rode her while I ran Mighty Mae around outside the fence. Jack was playing with Nibbles too. Hollyhock stayed calm!!

3. Afterward, Mr. Benson asked if I wanted to ride Hollyhock in the Parents Day demo tomorrow. WHAT??? I couldn't believe my ears! I asked if that meant she would get to stay at camp, and he said "She's doing well, but it's still too soon to tell."

Now I'm kind of worried about tomorrow. I have to make sure Hollyhock does everything perfectly during the demo. I have to prove that she's a GREAT camp horse!

Jack just caught me chewing on my pen. He asked if I was ner-cited about the demo. How'd he know? Then he turned one of my big sister tricks around on me. He said, "What are you most excited about?"

I said I'm excited about . . .
- showing everyone what a sweet, well-trained horse Hollyhock is.
- grooming her silky mane.
- showing Mom and Dad what I've learned about horses.

But while I thought about twinning with Hollyhock, I started missing Katie. We haven't talked in FOUR days—a new record. Will my best friend and I ever be okay again?

THURSDAY NIGHT

Tonight at gymnastics, I did what McKenna said—
I took a step back to a Silver skill. Instead of
jumping to the high bar, I jumped forward off the
low bar and landed on the mat. Avery said, "Nice
landing." I can tell she's trying to be a better
teammate.

I took a step back on beam too—I practiced my
cartwheel on the low beam instead of on the high
one. I looked toward the spot where I wanted to
land, and I . . . nailed it! If I can do a solid cartwheel
on the low beam, I know I can do one on the high

beam soon. I have to
keep boosting my
confidence until I'm
ready to take that
next step, just like
Hollyhock.

But during cooldown,
my worries started
creeping back in.
Emilia said it helps her
to say her worries out
loud, so I tried that.

I told her I was scared about what might go wrong during the Parents Day demo—that Hollyhock might spook.

Emilia's eyes got wide for a second, then she gave me a hug. "You'll be okay, Lila," she said. "You've been working with Hollyhock all week and you're a good rider. You've got this."

Avery heard what Emilia said and came over. "I bet you are a good rider, Lila. You're strong." Avery smiled at me, and I smiled back.

McKenna joined us, and she put her arm around my shoulder. "I believe in you, Lila. At the gym and in the arena."

I felt so supported by everyone, and at that moment, I felt like we were a team.

"Let's end practice with something fun," McKenna suggested.

FRIDAY, AUGUST 23

It's Parents Day, and I'm SO nervous. But I'm trying to stay calm for Hollyhock, because this is a huge day for her.

Emilia helped me brush Hollyhock until her coat shone like gold. Then I put colorful hair extensions into her mane and added some sparkly gems. She looks so pretty!

After I braided Hollyhock's tail, Emilia asked if I'd braid her hair too. While I was doing her hair, it almost felt like hanging out with Katie. I think I finally made a new friend, but my heart still misses my old one.

Other groups are doing demos for their parents right now, and I'm waiting by Hollyhock's stall. My stomach is doing cartwheels! It helps to journal about it, though. Jack is helping, too, by making me laugh. He's trying to groom Joker, but Joker keeps nibbling on Jack's shoelaces!

Freya said it's time to bring our horses into the arena. YIKES! Please, please, please let this go well for me—and especially for Hollyhock!

SADDLE UP

FRIDAY NIGHT

We just got home from Parents Day, and my mind keeps playing over every second.

When I led Hollyhock into the arena, I was so scared, I was shaking. But I had to act calm and confident so that she would feel confident, too.

I looked for my family in the audience. I saw Mom and Dad, and then I saw a girl in braids with a very familiar smile. Katie! She showed up to support me! When she waved at me, I felt this huge burst of courage.

Hollyhock must have felt it too, because when I nudged her to start walking, she practically pranced around that ring.

Suddenly someone in the audience took a photo with a flash (even though a sign on the barn door said not to). The other horses spooked, Ben stopped walking, Cinnamon snorted, and Joker stepped sideways. But I remembered everything Mr. Benson had taught me. I talked to Hollyhock in a soothing voice and gave her a reassuring pat, and she kept walking. She did GREAT!

After the demo, Katie showed me a video she took of me riding. "I get now why you like horse camp so much," she said. "You and Hollyhock were meant to be together."

Then Katie admitted that it's hard for her to see me doing new things without her, but that she wants to support me, even when it's hard.

"Hollyhock and I WERE meant to be together," I agreed with Katie, "just like you and I were meant to be best friends. And I really missed you at camp!"

Katie smiled. "You've missed me as much as I've missed you?" she said.

"Every single day," I said as we both stroked Hollyhock. Finally, it felt like things between us were okay again.

When it was time to go home, Jack had a hard time saying goodbye to his new furry friends. Just two weeks ago he was nervous about going to camp. Now he didn't want to leave!

I didn't want to leave either. Would Hollyhock still be here if I came back to visit? I went to say goodbye to her. When I looked into her big brown eyes, kissed her velvety nose, and breathed her sweet hay smell, my heart was full of love.

When she leaned into me, I couldn't bring myself to leave—even when Mom waved me toward the car. I stood there next to Hollyhock until Mr. Benson came over.

He said I'd done really well riding Hollyhock today. Then, FINALLY, he said the words I'd been longing to hear: "I think she will make a fine camp horse after all."

YESSS!!!

I gave Hollyhock another kiss and promised her I would come back and visit soon. When I turned to go, she watched me every step of the way. Then I was running down the hill to where Mom, Dad, Jack, and Katie were waiting.

MEET COACH MCKENNA

Since McKenna's been such a big part of my gymnastics journey, I asked her if I could interview her. Here's what I learned.

WHERE DID YOU GROW UP?
Seattle, Washington

HOW LONG HAVE YOU BEEN DOING GYMNASTICS?
Nineteen years. I started at Shooting Star Gymnastics when I was three years old, and I trained there until I moved to Minnesota.

YOU CAME HERE FOR COLLEGE, RIGHT?
Yes. I'm getting my degree in elementary education so I can be a teacher. I also started coaching gymnastics, which is a lot of fun.

WHAT'S YOUR FAVORITE GYMNASTICS EVENT?
It's a tie between the balance beam and the uneven bars. I've always felt strong and confident on the beam, but on the bars, I feel like I'm flying.

DID YOU HAVE ANY GOOD FRIENDS AT THE GYM?
Yes! I met Toulane Thomas on my first day in the Roly-Polies class. We were instant

McKenna, age 10, on the uneven bars

friends and went to school together, too. She was competitive, and she always pushed me to do my best.

My other good friend was Sierra Kuchinko. She was so flexible that I used to joke she was made of bungee cords. Sierra was a supportive teammate, and we encouraged each other through struggles and setbacks.

WHEN DID YOU BEGIN COMPETING?

When I was 10 years old, I moved to level four in gymnastics and started working on the skills I would need to join the competitive team. We had six months to train, and there were only two spots open. After a LOT of work, I made the team!

I BET THAT FELT AMAZING

It did—especially because of my injury!

REQUIRED ELEMENTS FOR LEVEL 4 COMPETITIVE TEAM

ON VAULT: handstand flat back onto a mat stack

ON BARS: glide swing, pullover, front hip circle, shoot-through, stride circle, single leg cut, cast, back hip circle to underswing dismount

ON BEAM: v-sit, heel-snap turn in coupé, leap, handstand, half turn in coupé, straight jump, tuck jump, scale, side handstand quarter-turn dismount

ON FLOOR: straight jump, split jump, handstand forward roll, handstand bridge kick-over, leap, hop, split, back roll to push-up position, half turn in coupé, round-off back handspring rebound

WHAT INJURY?

A few months before I made the competitive team, we did a demonstration for our families. It was the first time I'd performed in front of an audience, and I was nervous. During my dismount on the beam, I lost my balance and landed on the edge of my left foot.

WHAT HAPPENED?

I broke my ankle. I couldn't do gymnastics for almost three months.

HOW DID YOU SURVIVE?

Well, I still went to practice to stretch and to see what my teammates were doing. But I found out there were other things I liked to do, like write poetry. That's also when I started volunteering at Hearts and Horses, which is a horseback riding center for people with disabilities.

McKenna's dog, Cooper, was by her side while her ankle healed

HOW DID YOU LEARN ABOUT HEARTS AND HORSES?

A friend of mine—Josie—uses a wheelchair and wanted to learn how to ride a horse. She was nervous, so she asked me to come with her for support. I thought the center was awesome, and being there helped take my mind off my ankle and the stress of trying out for the competitive team. They needed volunteers, so I signed up. With school and gymnastics, I could only go for a few hours every other week, but working there gave me a sense of balance. It reminded me that there was room in my life for more than one interest.

THAT SOUNDS AMAZING. AND IT'S AMAZING THAT YOU GOT A SPOT ON THE COMPETITIVE TEAM AFTER BREAKING YOUR ANKLE.

I worked with a physical therapist who taught me exercises to stretch and strengthen my ankle, and I

Josie rode a sweet horse named Pumpkin

had to go slow at practice, so I didn't do too much too soon. It really helped that my coach said, "I believe in you. Now believe in yourself!"

WOW, MCKENNA. NOW I KNOW WHY YOU'RE SUCH A GREAT COACH. YOU'VE BEEN THROUGH IT ALL.

Aw, thanks, Lila. I love gymnastics, and coaching has given me a new way to appreciate the sport and the athletes.

SURPRISE!

MCKENNA BROOKS WAS THE 2012 GIRL OF THE YEAR!

Lila's Story Continues!

Does Lila make the Gold team?
Does she get to ride Hollyhock again?
Find out more in Lila's next book,
coming in January 2024.

Meet the Author, Illustrator, and Advisers

Erin Falligant took horseback riding lessons when she was a girl, just like Lila. But while Lila dreams of becoming a competitive gymnast, Erin dreamed of becoming an author—long before she wrote her first book. She has now written more than forty books for children, including contemporary fiction, historical fiction, advice books, and picture books. She has a master's degree in child clinical psychology and writes from her home in Madison, Wisconsin.

Vivienne To is an illustrator and concept artist. She has worked in the art department for several animated feature films, and her illustrations have been featured on many book covers and in many picture books. Vivienne lives in Wellington, New Zealand. When she isn't drawing, she can be found knitting on the couch, watching cute dogs at the local park, or getting lost in a good book.

Sarah Nelson is the business manager and head competitive gymnastics coach at Madtown Twisters Gymnastics in Madison, Wisconsin. She has coached gymnasts of all levels—from preschoolers to future collegiate athletes. She is also a nationally ranked gymnastics official and judges competitions all over the United States.

Ted Marthe is the co-owner of Hoofbeat Ridge Camps in Mazomanie, Wisconsin. He has directed both private and agency camps. Ted is the former executive director of the Horsemanship Safety Association, an organization dedicated to certifying horseback riding instructors and helping camps run safe horsemanship programs.

Visit **americangirl.com/play**
to discover more about Lila's world.

Look for bestselling books from
American Girl online and in stores.

Published by American Girl Publishing

23 24 25 26 27 28 29 QP 10 9 8 7 6 5 4 3 2 1

Written by Erin Falligant
Illustrations and cover image by Vivienne To
Book design by Gretchen Becker

Cataloging-in-Publication Data available from the Library of Congress

americangirl.com/service

Not all services are available in all countries.